KNUCKLES

NAUGHTY DEVILS MC BOOK 4

TILLY POPE

ABOUT KNUCKLES

Ava

My car broke down. My phone is dead, my pretty pink
boots are covered in mud and now it's going to rain.
I've got to get to a phone before dark.
I walk into a dive bar that has some seedy people inside.
I'm not afraid, I just need to use the phone.
Plus, I've got Mr. Snuggles to protect me.
Until this big, burly biker grabs me and *spanks* me!
So why am I so **turned on?**
And why do I want him to **do it again?**

Knuckles

After training hard, I've been kicking ass and taking
names.
Now, the Naughty Devil's MC won't take me on
anymore.
Chickens.
I head to the meanest biker bar on the outside of town
looking for some money and a fight.
When a cute little blonde walks in dressed head to toe in
pink with a tiny dog in her damn purse, I know the night
is about to get **interesting.**
The men in this place will eat her alive…so I find myself
protecting her.

I wonder what else the innocent damsel in distress will let me do?

Short, hot, and over the top! If you love bad boys, overly possessive alpha males, totally unrealistic instalove romance, (maybe even a bit cheesy) this one's for you! No cliffhanger, no cheating, and a guaranteed HEA!

For all my super yummy over the top readers!
Who's your daddy?

1
____

Ava

I glance over my shoulder, it's almost dark. My Lexus is already out of sight and I can't believe my bad luck.

I don't know what went wrong! My car was running fine, then it wasn't. So I did what I always do; I picked up my phone to call Dad. He'll drop everything and come help me like he always does.

But my phone only has three percent left. So I hit recent contacts and touch the last call, his number. It didn't even dial before the screen gave me the shutdown sequence and went black. Throwing my head back, I stare up at the darkening skies as a light, misting rain falls.

"Well this is ugly, isn't it Mr. Snuggles?" I glance into the pink tote at my Pomeranian. Beads of mist are clinging to his fluffy fur and he tucks into the bag with a slight whimper.

"We'll be okay." He needs assurance about everything, but I don't mind. The cold in the air settles into my skin and I shiver. My cute little dress is great for everything except hiking alongside the road, alone with my dog.

I continue what feels like a walk of shame. "We have the worst luck," I tell Mr. Snuggles. The bag shifts as he adjusts himself, and I move him to my other arm to ease some of the ache starting deep in my shoulder. It won't all be bad, though. When Dad hears about this, he'll likely send me on another vacation to make up for what I'm going through.

Maybe I'll go to Greece this time. Somewhere warm with beaches and good food. Somewhere I could work on my tan and get some bikini time in. Heck, maybe I'd even meet some handsome local and tour the city with him. No need to tell anyone I'd already been to Greece several times; sometimes it's nice to have a handsome man show you around.

The mist gets heavier and I feel my hair going limp. I'd gotten it styled this morning at the start of this stupid drive. "I must be a mess," I say to Mr. Snuggles, but he's ignoring me. I feel him shiver slightly in his bag and my heart aches for him.

"I shouldn't have made the trip this year," I say softly as he pokes his head out. His fluffy ears and inquisitive eyes bring a smile to my face. Maybe this is the year to stop my stupid tradition. Dad tries to talk me out of it every year. "I don't even know why I do this anymore. It doesn't make me happy. It changes nothing." Though, the drive calls to me and every year it takes me right back to that place.

I blink back tears and fan at my face. "I'm going to ruin my makeup!" I let out a shaky laugh, though I realize the rain is just as likely to mess up my face as my tears. Mr. Snuggles tilts his head at me, his long tongue disappearing into his mouth at the same moment.

My foot sinks into the mud and I stop. Glancing down at my foot, I see my pretty pink boot has sunk in a mud hole almost to my ankle. I pull it out, struggling not to lose my shoe. "These are my favorite boots!" I work my foot free with a gross suction sound and almost fall over.

I examine my once pink but now brown boot with a sigh. "At least I can see lights," I say to Mr. Snuggles. He lifts his head and sniffs toward the town and his tongue unrolls once more to hang out the right side of his mouth.

Done with all the things going wrong, I hurry toward the lights as fast as I dare. My heart sinks: the place is tiny. There's a diner that looks like it's already closed. A few shabby looking houses with the lights out.

"Is this place a ghost town?" I keep walking, letting my ears guide me toward the only noise I hear. Is that a bar? Maybe they have a phone. I'll go there.

After fifteen more minutes of walking, I reach the bar. There are a ton of motorcycles parked outside and I shiver. The place looks like they should condemn it. It's falling apart, the paint is mostly faded and peeled away; the sign is hand painted, and three of the four windows in front are broken, or have tiny holes in them.

"Well, I'm not getting a drink here," I say, looking at the building. With my heart pounding hard in my chest, I walk up to the front door. Pushing it open, I notice the whole place if full of men. Scary men with big bushy beards, hard, flat eyes, leather jackets and scowls.

I freeze in place. No doubt, this place is scary. But I need to call Dad. I just walked through the freezing cold and rain to get here, so I'm not going to turn around because there are some scary-looking men here.

I let out a long breath, With my chin held high, I walk toward the bar top. Like a wave following me, the conversations begin to die off and more eyes turn my direction. Mr. Snuggles pops his head out again and he yips at someone.

The guy lets out a mean sound and more attention turns toward us. But I'm so close to the bar I can almost touch it. Taking small breaths through my mouth, I try to ignore the smell. What is that? Vomit, man sweat, unwashed bodies, and booze, maybe? In all twenty of my years, I've never been in such a scary situation.

The sound of something solid hitting something with a thud pulls my attention and I notice two men are fighting. And there's blood on both of them! I've never seen two people fight before and that sound echoes through my brain.

Mr. Snuggles wiggles before popping out of my bag.

"No! Mr. Snuggles! Come back here!" I move toward him as he runs toward the fight.

"The fuck?" One man fighting lifts a foot as if he's going to stomp on my dog, but the other man's fist flashes out and hits the guy in the throat. Mr. Snuggles begins to bark at the fighting man, who hunkers down and offers his knuckles for my dog to sniff.

I see the guy he was fighting seem to recover and open my mouth to warn him. Before I can get a word out, the man scoops up Mr. Snuggles and turns him away from the man swinging at him. He takes the blow to the ribs and I scream.

Rushing over, I take my dog, aware that he took that hit to the ribs when he could have left my dog on the ground and knocked the other guy out. He'd protected Mr. Snuggles. Planting myself square between the men, I tell the other guy to stop.

He laughs at me and I glare at him.

"Here." The guy that saved my dog presses Mr. Snuggles to my chest and I tuck him into his tote. His hazel eyes meet mine and I notice the sweat clinging to his face and dampening his dark hair. He towers over me and there's something so dangerous about him my heart pounds.

Before I can say anything, I'm pulled out of the way and I realize the other man is continuing to fight with me standing in the way. I'm moved out of danger and the hazel-eyed man takes the other guy down with one hit.

I want to thank him for saving me, for saving Mr. Snuggles, but I need to escape. Rushing to the bar, I open my mouth. "I need to borrow your phone."

2

Knuckles

The little spitfire had tried to stand up for me… and almost got taken the fuck out by the asshole I'd just put down like the fucking dog he is.

I saw the fear in her eyes as her little dog ran up to me. And I saw that the fucker I was fighting wanted to kill the damn dog. But what could the little puffball do to hurt either of us? He was about the size of a spitball.

I wasn't about to let anything happen to the little mutt. Not because I give a damn about this particular dog, but because I have three rules; don't hurt women, don't hurt kids, don't hurt animals.

"Good win." Some old bastard claps me on the back.

I nod without taking my eyes off the woman in pink. She doesn't belong here. I can see that, and everyone around me seems fixated on that same detail. Every man in the room is staring at her like they have a hard on for her, and not the pleasant, she might like it kind either. They're looking at her like they want to fuck her up. And that pisses me off more.

She's clearly a spoiled little brat with her pink everything and tiny little fluffy dog in a purse, and she came walking into a rough biker bar without a thought in the world about it. Still, a second glance shows that she's been walking in the rain, one of her shoes is covered in mud, and her makeup is all over her face., and I have a feeling it was perfect before whatever happened to her.

And her plucky attitude—I can't believe she tried to stand up for me in the middle of a fight—tells me that whatever bad things have happened to her tonight; they haven't broken her.

"Your money." A hand presses my winnings into my palm and I take the wad of bills with a nod, still not taking my eyes off her. Everything about this young woman screams privilege, from her expensive clothing to the jewelry gracing her throat, ears, and fingers. Her perfect blonde hair is elegantly styled despite being wet from the elements, and her artic blue eyes with their dark fringe of lashes don't seem to notice the danger closing in on her.

Someone bumps her arm and she glares at the beefy guy. I recognize the troublemaker from a rival club and something in me tightens. I'm not going to walk away and let bad things happen to this young woman.

It's not my business. But I won't stand by and let this happen. Damn my rules.

I push my way past the group even as someone challenges me to double or nothing match. I could make a killing in cash tonight; my reputation hasn't caught up to the training I've done so everyone thinks my win was a fluke. I'm walking away from a lot of money… but I'm not sure I'll sleep tonight if this young woman winds up in a ditch somewhere because some asshole here wants to teach her—and every woman like her—a lesson.

I'm not a fucking hero, but I have a conscience.

Fuck. "Maybe another night," I say.

"Deal expires in five minutes."

"What, you only brave for the next five minutes?" I continue walking toward the bar, not giving a shit that I'm pissing people off. I already know how this night is going to end and I'm already bruised. What's one more fight?

Her lip curls a bit and I know she's about to say something to the guy next to her that's not going to go over well. I recognize that look of disgust and I'm sure the guy she's aiming the expression at recognizes it too.

She's going to get herself killed. The guys in this dive bar aren't friendly people.

I drop onto the barstool next to her. "Hey little sis, what are you doing here?" I can only hope that our interaction earlier will help sell my story.

She glances at me, then leans away. The recognition in her eyes as they sweep up and down me isn't enough to take the disgust out of her expression and I tuck the wad of cash into my pocket. Winding an arm around her shoulders, I pull her close even as she tries to pull away. "If you want to make it out of here alive, play along."

I nod at the guy next to her, then calmly order a double shot of Jack.

I've thrown out the gauntlet. Every motherfucker in this place knows that if they mess with her, they're also messing with me.

The bartender places my drink in front of me and I knock it back quickly, ignoring the flaming pain in my ribs where I took the hit earlier. Her little dog licks my arm and I stare into those brown puppy dog eyes wondering what the hell the little critter wants.

I'm sure as hell not going to hold or pet the little bastard. It gives a tiny whimper and I shush it, knowing that drawing more attention to her is not a good idea right now. Getting another drink, I gulp it as she stares at the guy next to her. His bitter glare and hatred are obvious. The sneer on his face tells us both exactly what he wants to do to her and I feel her tremble with fear beside me.

She turns back my direction, her wide artic blue eyes filling with fear.

And it hits me, she doesn't want to be here. Hell, her expression says she'd rather be anywhere but here.

Well, sweetheart, this isn't how I want to spend my night either. And it's about to get a lot worse.

3
____

*A*va

The smell of the guy's alcohol infused breath is stinging my nose and I glare at him. I don't know who he is or what he's trying to pull, but I'm not falling for his weird come on.

I plant a hand on my hip and come at him with every bit of sass I possess. "I don't even know you."

He hangs his head a bit and his hair falls forward to frame his forehead. "I wish you hadn't said that," he says softly. There's something so ominous in his words that my heart sinks. Still, I don't feel like he'd hurt me, but why would he say that? The scent of man sweat tickles my nose, and he's kind of hot.

My voice rises. "I've never seen you before in my life!" I don't care that the guy on the other side of me is staring like he wants to cut me up, stuff me into a duffel bag, and make me disappear. I'm sure there are other good people here that need to know that this guy is lying. I'm not his sister or his friend. And if I go missing like some girl on a true crime show, I need witnesses that remember this event.

But as I look around the room, I realize this crowd likely wouldn't talk to cops if they came looking for me. I'm reasonably certain everyone here is a criminal. Fear pounds in my ears as the guy orders another drink.

Tension fills the room so thick I can hardly breathe, and Mr. Snuggles begins to whine.

"Shut that rat up." The guy next to me is so angry, so gruff I stare at him in disbelief.

"He's just scared," I say.

"He's a fucking dog. Dogs fight, they don't get scared and cry like a little fuckin' pussy." Someone else is speaking and I try to find the owner of the voice. Is everyone moving closer to me? I'd swear they're closing in.

My whole body jolts as the guy next to me slams his empty glass down on the bar. "Thank you," he says to the bartender, sliding some bills across the counter.

"I'm just here to use the phone. Please let me make a call, then I'll leave." I try pleading with the bartender, but he's ignoring me. Mr. Snuggles lets out a sharp yip and the surrounding men react as if they've been stabbed, or whatever makes burly guys like them stiffen up suddenly.

The mean guy next to me begins to crack his knuckles while someone else lets out a low growl. I glance behind me again, certain this time that they are closing in around me. They are absolutely closer than they were last time I looked. But why are all these black leather clad bikers approaching me?

I gently squeeze Mr. Snuggles as if I can stop him from barking by cuddling him close. It only seems to upset him more, and he begins to bark. All around the guys make angry noises and start to do things like roll their necks, crack their knuckles, and move distressingly closer to me.

"Can I please use the phone?" I ask again, very real terror surging in my chest. What are these criminals going to do if I don't get out of here? Mr. Snuggles continues to bark, the bartender is still ignoring me, and I slip a hand in my purse. Without thinking twice, I pull out my pepper spray and hold it up.

"Back off!" I shout at everyone, sweeping the room with my pepper spray at the ready. "I'll mace you all, damn it."

Silence falls—even Mr. Snuggles seems to get the hint that I'm serious and quiets down—and I continue to watch as the angry mob halts in place.

The man that called me sister is still sitting, his head partially down, not even looking at me. Other than that, everyone in the room seems focused on me.

Then the mean guy next to me laughs.

As if on cue, the other man stands, winds an arm around my shoulders, and ushers me toward the door. As I try to fight, he holds me tighter with arms that feel like steel. How strong is this man? *Tough guy much?*

He could snap me in half if he wanted to…and for some reason that thought makes my cheeks burn.

Fighting to get away from the guy holding me captive, I stomp on his toe. He doesn't so much as blink at my attempt. I dig an elbow into his ribs, trying to pry him off me. But he clings with a grip so tight I can hardly breathe, and I know I can't get away from him. Why doesn't he let me go?

And why is there a strange warmth washing through me? Am I into this stuff?

Not knowing what else to do, I depress the trigger on my pepper spray. Men start shouting, coughing, and fists begin flying. In moments, the whole room is erupting in fistfights as everyone devolves into Neanderthals, hell bent on destruction, fighting and burning the place to the ground.

We slip outside in the rain and I try to reason with my captor. What's the first rule of being kidnapped? Humanize yourself? "If I don't get home, it'll kill my mom and dad." As I think about my parents, tears fill my eyes, but I blink them back. "And my friends will be heartbroken…" I think about my friends and a lump threatens to cut off the air to my lungs.

I glance up at the man, but he doesn't respond. Or even look at me. So I switch tactics. "My dad will pay for my safe return. He'll pay whatever you want."

That seems to get his attention. He stops, stares at me with his lip curled in disgust, and I blink. "You need to shut the fuck up."

But a second later he's dragging me away again and my heart begins to thunder in my chest.

Obviously, he's more interested in raping and murdering me than he is getting paid to keep me safe. I saw the wad of money he stuffed in his pocket. No doubt he's a drug dealer or something just as undesirable. Maybe he doesn't want or need my dad's money.

God, why did I come here?

"He'll pay you whatever you want," I say again, in case he didn't hear me. "Just keep me safe until he can send someone to come get me." I'm begging with this stranger to not only *not* hurt me but keep me safe for a short while. And he's not even acknowledging a word I say. What is wrong with this guy? "Please?" I beg, hating the tears that begin to sting in my eyes.

Seemingly out of nowhere, three men cut off our escape. We stop dead in our tracks and the ringleader— the same jerk who was sitting next to me in the bar— steps forward.

I want to back up a step and put more distance between us, but the stranger's arm around me holds me in place. Mr. Snuggles raises his barks to almost screeching and then the ringleader glares bitterly at my dog, then set his sights on me. Oh, my God. Is he going to kill my dog?

"We'll take you up on that offer," he says with a sinister grin and grabs his crotch and wiggles it. His demeanor makes my stomach turn and my heart stop beating in my chest.

4

—————

nuckles

Fuck.

Of course she wouldn't get the hint to stop talking about her dad's money. Doesn't she realize how much danger she's in right now? Or how much more danger her money talk is going to get us in?

I size up the guys in front of us. Good thing I had a few drinks before coming out here, because I know this is going to fucking hurt. I also know I can kick their sorry asses.

The guy to the right rushes me. I push the woman aside and take him out with a single jab to the throat. He collapses to his knees, grabbing his throat and gasping for air. With every wheeze he makes, I feel his friends getting more and more angry with me.

The other guy approaches with more caution. I see the glint of something metal in his hand and the woman cries out. I glance at her only to see she's looking at the knife. The guy takes advantage of my split attention and lunges. I leap back, but not before I feel the bite of cold steel. With a grin, he approaches again, the ringleader circling my other side.

"Why are you sticking up for this bitch?" the ringleader asks.

Because sticking up for a woman is better than being a flaming douchebag.

"We could split the money." He glances at her. "How much would your daddy give us? How much would he pay to make sure you got home alive and…" he lets his eyes travel down her body, then slowly back up, *"safe?"* His tongue traces his lower lip and I want to beat the fuck out of him.

She backs up a step. "Um, I don't know how much exactly, but he'd make it worth your while." Her voice trembles slightly and I know this motherfucker is getting off on scaring her.

"See, her daddy would make it worth our while," he says, glancing at me. "So how about it? Are you with us?"

Fury fuels me and I throw a mean right hook in his direction. My knuckles connect with his jaw and I hear the sickening sound of bones giving way. Pain flares through my hand and side, and the bastard falls to the ground. His hands fly up to his jaw and I realize that it's sideways and he can't seem to fix it.

She screams and I leap for her, trying to turn her away as her little dog starts yapping again.

The second guy races toward me and I guide her toward my bike before knocking the knife wielder to the ground. Despite the adrenaline coursing through me like the best drug, I feel my strength beginning to wane and I leave the guy on the ground before hauling her toward my bike.

She fights me every step of the way until I'm nearly dragging her.

"You really want to stay here with them?" I ask, knowing I don't have a lot of time left. I need to get us both the fuck out of here before there's no chance of escape. Thrusting a hand toward the guys that just threatened to hold her hostage for ransom and rape her. The first guy seems to have passed out, the ringleader is preoccupied with how he'll be drinking through a straw for a while, but the knife guy, he's on the verge of coming for me again. And if he gets that blade on my skin again, there might be no getting away.

She struggles less as I pull her toward my bike, but I can sense her fear and worry. "What are you going to do?" she asks, but there's something else in her voice. An excitement that twists up my insides.

"Get you somewhere safe." Then pass the fuck out. Not that I'm going to admit that part to her. Thank God for booze—I can't feel the pain. I make it to my bike and sit, but she's still hesitant and pulls back a bit.

Suddenly done fighting with her—and aware how much is at stake—I grab her and pull her across my lap, across the bike seat. Before I can stop myself, my hand flies and connects with her sexy rounded ass. I watch the bounce of her ass in the wake of my smack, a satisfied feeling fills my core. I spank her right here on my bike.

She glances over her shoulder at me. Her face is beet red, her eyes wet, and those perfect lips part in a sexy smile as heat fills her expression. Fuck yeah. She likes it.

Frozen in place, with her dog purse swinging softly from her shoulder close to the ground, I breathe a sigh of relief.

Fuck if I don't want to spank her ass again, though. Damn it, that's not even a fetish I thought I had, but something told me she needed a firm hand. No doubt she'd been pampered, babied, and treated like a porcelain doll all her life. Probably got a few participation trophies as well.

"I'm going to take you somewhere safe. Now you better get on this damn bike before he decides to fuckin' kill us." I nod at the knife guy who's checking on his friends while glancing at me over his shoulder like he's trying to decide if we're worth it or not. She stands up beside the bike and stares at me.

"You just... spanked me." Her humiliated whisper holds a hint of excitement.

"I did." I arch an eyebrow at her. "And I'll do it again if you don't listen to me, woman." I don't think I'm smarter than anyone else, but right now she's being stupid and childish and I'm going to smack her ass again if she doesn't stop staring at me and get on this damn bike, *now*. But only for that reason, of course, not because I want to spank her again.

I mean, I do want to spank her again because that was fucking hot, but…

She hesitates.

"*Now*."

But she's not moving. I decide it's time to give her another more pressing reason to get moving. I pull my leather vest aside, then peel the black tee shirt from my rib, wincing a little as I do so. Staring down at the spot, I know I should be feeling pain, but I don't. Little by little, I reveal the bloody gash where he'd slashed me.

"Oh my God," she whispers, pressing her hands to her face.

I gently probe the wound, fascinated that it doesn't hurt. Deep in the torn up gouge I see bone and her eyes widen.

"Get on the damn bike so I can get some medical attention." Fresh blood seeps down my abs and I see her taking in every inch of my flesh with arousal in her eyes. This horny little bi—

"Okay." She climbs on the back of my bike in a hurry.

I turn over the engine and we roar out of the parking lot in a shower of gravel as I cling to consciousness. Behind us, I see the knife guy come running, but he's too late to catch us and no doubt his friends need medical attention too.

Her arms tighten around me, one above and one below my wound. Her palms press flat and I know she's feeling me up. I don't have the energy to be outraged—or turned on. I can feel myself fading as I drive.

I make every turn out of sheer muscle memory alone, though the short ride to the club is almost more than I can take. Through sheer force of will, I stay awake as we bump over the curb and into the club's parking lot.

It takes every bit of strength I have to put down the kickstand… and then everything goes black.

5

Ava

He seems to be fine until his chin drops to his chest and his body falls. Two guys leap forward and grab him; one takes his shoulders, the other lifts his ankles and they carry him inside while a woman ushers me in.

I think she said her name was Haley, but she disappears after bringing me inside.

I'm perched on the edge of a loveseat stained with goodness knows what and wait for some news. Mr. Snuggles gives a slight whimper, and I offer him a gentle rub. Someone in the main room shouts, making me jolt, and there's an uproar that sounds like a fight.

I try to hide the shaking of my hands as I sit and wait. He said I'll be safe here, but I'm not so sure. I don't even know his name.

My cheeks grow warm as I think about the strange

burst of heat that exploded through me when he pulled me across his lap and spanked me. My butt is still on fire.

I think I'm *turned on by him*. Which is impossible. I mean, he's a biker, a criminal, a thug. I've never even broken the law. I may have sped a few times, but those laws don't count. I'm not like him.

"Hey little Miss."

I nearly jump out of the filthy seat as an old biker appears at my elbow. Maybe if I ignore him, he'll go away.

"What's your name?" He sits down beside me and I scoot away a few inches.

"Are you one of them hard-of-hearing folks?" He gestures and I peek at him out of the corner of my eye. I see he's missing an arm. And he grins at me while I face forward again. "I can't do any signing without righty."

I swallow hard and try my best to stare through the door like some teleportation trick. It doesn't work. There's a good-sized gap under the door and I have half a mind to dive for it and try to wiggle under.

He lowers his voice and leans toward me like he's about to impart some secret. "Want me to tell you how I lost my arm?"

I absolutely do *not*.

Gritting my teeth, I continue staring at the door. If my biker savior doesn't wake up soon, I might just run for the next place that might let me make a call. Still, it doesn't feel right to run—he saved my life and got hurt trying to protect me. Surely, I owe him something.

I sigh. If Daddy was here, he'd help me figure out what to do next.

"It's a good story. And it was a good thing I lost my right arm too, because I shoot with my left." The man chuckles and I shudder at the sound. He shoots people. And he's comfortable telling me, a total stranger, that he shoots people. I try to scoot away a little more but Mr. Snuggles protests my movement with a whine.

Without warning, Mr. Snuggles jumps out of his carrier and scampers across the floor. I watch in horror as he slips through the gap under the door. With a gasp, I leap to my feet and rush the door. I turn the knob and push my way inside. The biker that saved me from the bad guys that wanted to do awful things to me sat on a chair not unlike the tattoo chair my friend Alice had sat on when she snuck out and got ink. I should have gotten a little tattoo with her, like that super cute little octopus one I loved.

This place looks like a makeshift hospital room. There is a cabinet with what looks like pills in it, and a hospital bed.

"Don't get used to this," The biker says, "I'm just drugged up." He scratches Mr. Snuggles behind the ears even as he glances up at me in surprise.

The man braces his hands on the arm rests and pushes himself up into a sitting position. I see the white bandage wrapped around his ribs and I gasp.

"Are you okay?" I ask, stepping closer.

"Better now," he says. He reaches out his bruised hand

to shake mine. "I'm Knuckles, by the way."

Knuckles. His name is *Knuckles*. Who names their kid Knuckles?

But he saved my life. "I'm Ava." I say as I shake his calloused hand.

"Ava." He says my name and a shiver tickles down my spine. Mr. Snuggles—the traitor—jumps up into Knuckles' lap and stares at me. His ears perk up.

"I'm sorry you got hurt. Thank you for saving me from those creeps." Even though this place isn't the most savory, he was right; no one tried to hurt me. I lean over and press a kiss to his lips without a second thought about what I'm doing.

Warmth floods my being, and I let out a sigh before kissing him again. That same buzz of heat and excitement tingle along every nerve ending. I enjoy kissing him. Almost as much as I like him spanking me. Maybe if I kiss him again, he'll spank me again. After he heals, I mean.

The corners of his lips curve into a smile as he glances over my shoulder. I turn and see the other biker give Knuckles a wink before closing the door.

"I take it SawedOff talked to you?" he asks with an arched eyebrow.

I nod, assuming that SawedOff—his name is *SawedOff?* I'm glad I didn't let him tell me his story!—is the older dude missing an arm.

Knuckles chuckles. "That's his way of trying to make you feel better. He doesn't tell everyone his story, so if he offered to tell you, it's a sign that he's trying to help you feel more comfortable."

He was trying to help me. I pause, stunned by the revelation. I've spent this whole time assuming the kind of people these bikers are, yet this one saved my life, the girl made me feel comfortable up until she disappeared inside chasing after some tall bear of a man, and the older guy was apparently trying to help me. Maybe I've had them all wrong from the start.

I glance at Mr. Snuggles and notice he's curled into the biker's side. My dog is dozing off as if he doesn't have a care in the world and I can't hold back a smile.

"So why did you wind up in that bar?" Knuckles asks.

"I needed to call my dad." My heart is racing. Maybe this entire ordeal is nearing the end.

"Oh, you can use my phone." He pulls it out of his pocket and offers it to me. I stare at it. After how hard everything has been since my car broke down, this seems too easy.

"Why were you at the bar?" I ask, suddenly curious.

He gives me a heart-stopping grin. "I was looking for a fight."

Of course he was. But am I really ready for this to end? I'm curious about this biker and the strange tingling excitement I feel in his company. I really want to kiss him again, too.

And the more I think about it, the more I realize that maybe these rough-looking guys aren't all bad... are they?

6

$\mathcal{K}$nuckles

I know that SawedOff locked the door on his way out, and I know exactly what the old bastard had in mind. Not that I'm against the idea of banging this sexy woman in pink, I just can't help but think maybe I'm not her type.

She's probably into some boring ass stuffed suit that rakes in a cool million a year. None of which I am.

"I like kissing you," she whispers. There's something so innocent, sweet, and pure about her. My cock stands at attention. I wonder if she's a virgin.

"I like when you kiss me." While we're sharing truths, I have another. "I also enjoyed spanking you."

Her eyes widen and her cheeks go red—which is all the evidence I need to know that she also enjoyed my hand across her ass. As much fun as it would be to take her in this room, I worry she's the kind of good girl that needs a bed and likely expects me to stick to the boring missionary position until I come and she's left unsatisfied…just a hunch.

Her little dog leaps to its feet to dance around me as I sit up with effort. The drugs they gave me for pain are great; I don't feel shit. But I am a little high. Nothing I can't get through.

"Let's get out of here." I scoop up her little dog and tuck him into my vest pocket. He curls right in, leaving me looking like I've suddenly acquired a beer gut. Ava seems stunned.

"You're injured, shouldn't you stay right here?" She scans the room like it's a top-notch hospital room and I chuckle.

"Let's go, sweetheart." I take her hand and lead her out of the room. She follows me through the club toward the private rooms. I take her to mine and close and lock it behind us. Without a word, I turn to face her.

She rises on tiptoes to press a kiss to my lips. Between us, her little dog yelps and she jerks back with a soft apology. I pull the squirming pup out and set him on the floor. He's off sniffing around as she winds her arms around my shoulders.

"He likes you," she whispers.

I shrug. "He's okay."

She laughs and I kiss her. Swallowing her gasp of surprise, I deepen the kiss. Backing up carefully, I sit down on the edge of my bed and pull her onto my lap.

She straddles me, her heart thundering so hard I feel it against my chest.

Grabbing her hips, I begin to rock her a bit, grinding our bodies together in a rhythm as old as time. I want her more than I think I've ever wanted any woman. Which is ridiculous. She's not my type, I'm sure as fuck not hers. But this feels right and I'm not going to stop until I figure out why…or she asks me to stop.

She inhales as I break the kiss.

"Tell me what you like," I growl.

Heat flushes her cheeks. "Um… I liked…" her voice drops to a humiliated whisper, "the spanking."

I stare her in the face until she meets my gaze. "No need for embarrassment. I'm sure as fuck not going to judge you."

She winces, then seems to see me for the first time. Her gaze traces my face, my neck, my shoulders, then comes back to meet mine as her little dog curls up next to my bed and begins to snore and twitch almost instantly. Her tongue races across her lower lip, leaving a slight sheen behind.

She kisses me this time. Our tongues meet and she pulls her purse off her shoulder and sets it down. As we break the kiss, I lean in to taste her neck and her pink jacket slides down her slim arms, leaving her in her pink dress. I stare at her. This girl can make anything sexy, even pink. Her blonde hair falls down around her shoulders and those incredible blue eyes meet mine as her teeth tug her lower lip.

"Stand up," I growl.

She does so without hesitation and I grab her and pull her across my lap. Her gasp is music to my ears and I work her dress up her thighs and over her perfect ass. The pink lace thong is such a delicate scrap of cloth I grab and give it a good yank.

It breaks in my hand and she gasps, glancing over her shoulder at me as I drop the lace on the floor. With one hand, I rub the smooth skin of her ass cheek before giving it a sharp smack. And then another. The perfect pink flesh is bright red and I slap that ass again. My cock twitches in my pants and I smile. I've never had such perfection. Soft, pink. Innocent.

Ava lets out a sexy ass whimper.

"Good?" I ask.

She nods, and I see how flushed her cheeks are. She's really enjoying this. But there are other things I want to do. I scoop her up and bring her across my lap again. She straddles me, her hips grinding on their own this time. "I want you to fuck me," she whispers.

I nod and her eyes widen.

Ava slides off my lap, unbuttons my pants and works the zipper down. Her smooth fingers slide under my boxers and I slip out of my vest, wondering why the hell they cut half of my shirt off to tend my wound but left me in my vest. *Dumbfucks.*

She wraps her slim, soft fingers around my cock and I fight back the urge to lift her up and fuck her hard.

Instead, I slip out of my pants and pull her into my lap. Her dress hits the floor and I adjust.

With her perfect tits on display, I can't help but claim one with my mouth. I suck that pert pink nipple deeply and she cries out. "Harder!"

Her sweet smell and warm skin leave me wanting more and I try to remind myself that she's not likely to have been with anyone as rough as me. She may not realize what *harder* means to a biker like me. I need to be gentle with her, this first time at least.

Because this won't be the last time.

Without missing a beat, she raises up and then slides down on my cock. Taking me in one firm, swift motion.

She's pleasantly wet and slick. Did spanking her make her this wet?

I growl and she clings to me; her whisper tickling my ear. "I haven't done this a lot."

"I figured," I say, my hands gripping her hips. "That's why we're going to make it count. Did you like my mouth on your nipple?"

She whimpers in response and I lick the taut pink nipple that's still red from my mouth before moving to the other side. Her gaze stays locked on mine as I take her in my mouth. I pull gently as her hips buck. Flicking my tongue across her nipple, I ask again. "Do you like this?"

I'm not going to let her refuse to answer.

Sucking her tit again, I watch her head fall back as she lets out a gasp of stunned surprise. "Yes!"

Suddenly, she's moving. Her whole body shakes, her hips bouncing wildly on my cock. I hold on to her. Ava can't weigh 100 pounds soaking wet and as slick as she is, I don't want her bouncing away.

"I love that," she whispers, though I'm not sure what she's talking about. The dam seems to have burst and she's riding me hard. Goose bumps break out across every inch of her skin and I release her nipple before giving them both a kiss and a lick, respectively.

"Do you like riding my cock?" I ask, trailing my tongue between her tits toward the base of her throat.

"Mmmhmm," she whimpers, now grinding in circles. I can't believe she takes this ten inch cock with vigor. Yes, I'm blessed. Her walls clench tighter and I know she's on the edge. Damn, she wasn't kidding.

"You're going to come all over me, aren't you?" I scrape my teeth on her shoulder and she yelps.

"I like that. I like what you do with your mouth." Her words seem to add to her pleasure and I can tell she enjoys talking about how turned on she is.

"What else do you like, kitten?" I slide one hand behind her back, then lower. Slipping a slippery finger in her asshole to the second knuckle, I feel her jerk in stunned surprise. She doesn't stop riding me, though. "Ahh, you like that, too?"

"Yes!" Her quick, gasping breaths turn me on more. She's losing herself to me, to the pleasure we're sharing, and that's more intoxicating than any alcohol I've ever drank. Her sweat and warmth press around me so tight I nearly see stars, and I feel her give in to the orgasm.

Every muscle in her body tightens and she lets out a stunned, shuddering breath. She slams her ass down on my finger and juices flood out of her cunt. My cock pulses when she lets out a growl so long and loud, I'm afraid the dog's going to howl.

I need to kiss her again. I want to lose myself in her. No warning, no chance to act or react, I fill her full of my own slick pleasure as she clings to me, catching her breath.

Holding her close, I inhale her sweet scent as our hearts hammer in our chests so hard it's impossible to tell where hers begins and mine ends.

"Oh, my God. It's never been that good," she whispers.

I chuckle and brush her hair off her shoulder. "I'll fuck you like that anytime, kitten. Just say the word."

Her cheeks turn red and I press a kiss to her warm skin. A slight noise draws our attention and we glance over to see her dog, still sleeping, snoring like an old man. She giggles and I hold her tight, swearing to myself that I'm never going to let her go. *She's mine now.*

7

———

*a*va

I wake up to Knuckles propped up on an elbow beside me, studying my face. With a smile and a stretch, I yawn.

"How are you this morning?" I touch his abs just below the injury to his ribs. We'd redressed it last night, and I'd gotten my first lesson in first aid. And I was kind of good at it, surprisingly.

"Not too bad." But his grimace tells me otherwise.

I roll over and grab a pill off the table before offering it to him. He gives me a confused glance. "How did you get painkillers?"

I smile, thinking about what I'd done. "Well, let's just say Mr. Snuggles got loose in the infirmary and in the chaos, some pills fell into my pocket."

He stares at me. "You stole pain meds?"

I nod, swallowing hard. He doesn't look happy. "Did I screw up?" I ask.

But he chuckles. "No, but you could have just asked one of the girls for the meds. They know you're with me and that I'm hurt."

"Oh." I bite down on my lower lip as he grabs my chin between his index finger and thumb, tugging me closer for a kiss. Our lips meet and again, I realize I don't want to leave. I have to admit, hearing him say that everyone knows I'm with him makes me warm and fuzzy inside.

We part and he takes the pill while I grab my phone. Daddy is going to be so upset. I'd charged my phone and now it's at one hundred percent, but I didn't call last night and I'm dreading calling today.

"Just call him, kitten. He's bound to be worried about you." Despite Knuckle's calming tone, I can't shake the fear rising in me.

I know he'll be worried. What I don't know is how to tell him why I'm not coming home yet. With a deep breath, I call him.

He picks up on the first ring. "Ava! Where are you? Are you okay?"

"I'm fine, Daddy. My phone went dead." I sit up, remember I'm naked, and my face flames as I wrap the blankets around myself.

"Why didn't you charge it?" His worry breaks my heart and I wish I'd called sooner.

"My car broke down. But it's okay. I'm okay." I glance

at Knuckles, who smiles and gently touches my cheek. Tingling heat flares in me and I lean into his touch.

"Broke down? Need me to send someone, honey?" His voice softens.

I shake my head while answering. "No, I'm okay. I'll get it fixed here in town in the next few days."

"Are you sure? I know how hard this time of year is for you. I could drive out there right now."

I smile and shake my head. "No, I'm okay. Really. I'm not rushing the trip this year." At this point, I don't think I'll even finish the trip this year. For the first time, I have no desire to make the drive and where there'd been pain before, I now feel peace.

"Okay. You have your credit card?" His tone has softened even more.

"I do. Thank you, Dad. I appreciate you. I'll check in regularly." I know I'm smiling like an idiot, but I expected him to be disappointed or upset by my news. Not understanding and supportive.

"You better. No more radio silence. And call me if you need anything. *Anything.* I love you." Something like pride lights up his voice and I promise myself I'll take some time to figure out what is going through his head too, but now is not the time.

"Of course. And you can call me too, you know." I'm teasing. I know he called a dozen times.

He laughs and we say our goodbyes before hanging up.

I turn to Knuckles. His expression is warm and something in his eyes feels like coming home. 'I have the strangest feeling that everything is changing."

He nods. "I know what you mean."

"But nothing has changed." Not really.

But he chuckles. "Everything has changed. You called him Dad. Not Daddy. You also told him you'd take care of something that he's always had to take care of for you before. You're on your own, taking care of your own problems."

I suck in a deep breath. He's right. I've never had to do anything for myself before. "You're right," I say. There's something else I want to talk about too. "Why did you save me at the bar?"

He seems surprised by my question, but answers in a soft voice that has my heart fluttering. "I wanted to do the right thing. There were some bad people there for sure, and they wanted to do ugly things to you."

"And you don't want to do ugly things to me?" I smile, knowing full well where this conversation is going to lead.

"Oh, I do." The wicked gleam in his eyes has my body ready to go. It's strange, really. Yesterday, I was certain all bikers are criminals. That these people were the kind I needed to stay away from. But Knuckles surprised me. So did SawedOff. So did everyone else here. I don't fit in to this crazy crowd, but I feel at home here.

And I can see myself falling for this man. Really falling for him, too.

He leans in and kisses me. "I want to do bad, ugly

things to you," he growls and my heart thunders in my chest.

"I can't wait," I whisper as he kisses me again.

I kiss him, unable to hold back a smile.

"I'm sorry I ruined your trip," he says.

But he didn't. Someday I'll tell him the trip was my way of honoring a lost friend. A dear friend who'd lost her life when we were sixteen when a truck slid on the ice and slammed into her car. I'd been in the passenger seat. Fate spared me. Or so I thought. Now I wonder if that accident led me to be afraid to live. Afraid to do anything for myself. Maybe I've been stuck at sixteen all this time. Not anymore.

"You didn't ruin anything. I'm right where I want to be. For now."

"For now?" he has the grace to sound worried.

"For now." I'm not going to rush anything. But I'd like to see where things can go between us.

EPILOGUE

Knuckles

Four months later...

I glance at her in her pink get up. It's been four months since that first crazy romp with her and it's been a hell of a ride. I have to admit, I'm a little sad that our unprotected session didn't end up with her pregnant, but it's for the best, I'm sure.

I'll keep it to myself that the thought of her pregnant with my child is something I want and secretly hope for. That's not all I want from her, either.

She smiles at me and Mr. Snuggles bolts out of her purse to run and jump at me. I catch the crazy little dog and tuck him in my vest. He pokes his head out and his tongue hangs crazily to the side as he stares at the bikers around us. While Ava talks to Haley in some private little conversation the two seem lost in, I chuckle at the stories happening around me.

Mika sits on Viking's lap as Mace talks. At Mace's side, Lorelei stands in her leathers. Her stance dares anyone to come talk to her, and I can't help but be happy for my friends.

"If love is an illness, we're all infected," Blade says as Sunny pinches the bridge of her nose between her thumb and index finger.

"It seems to be going around." Several people glance at me even as SawedOff speaks up next.

"I'll take bets on who's next."

Instantly bets start getting placed and I laugh.

"Does he count?" Joker jerks his head toward me.

"He's already a lost cause, so no bets on him." SawedOff winks at me.

I'm a lost cause? I guess I am. I glance at Ava. I haven't told her yet, but I'm in love with her. I keep telling myself I'll come clean with her, but every time I try to say the words, something chokes me out.

She arches an eyebrow at me, her white, even teeth flashing in the low light. As Haley says something, she's suddenly back to attentive mode and I imagine she's comforting her friend. A moment later, she gives Haley a hug and heads my direction while bets are still being called. I can see fingers pointing at others around the club, but I'm focused on the woman I love walking toward me.

Without a word, she leans into me and presses her lips to mine.

"Has he said it yet?" Someone asks, still demanding to bet on me as SawedOff refuses to take them on.

"Said what?" Ava glances at me, wide-eyed.

"Ignore them. They're taking bets on who'll fall in love next."

Her face lights up. "Oh! I'm in." She gestures and SawedOff nods at her.

"Did you really just…" She's over here taking fuckin bets on who'll fall in love next.

With a laugh, she kisses me again. "Sorry, was I supposed to bet on us? Because I already know I love you."

"And I love you." The words feel right rolling off my tongue and she lights up.

"Really?" she asks.

"Really." I want to spend the rest of my life with this woman… if she'll have me.

"Well," she says, "Then, I guess it's time for you to meet Dad."

I'm not ready for that. "Who'd you bet on?" I ask her.

She laughs. "Are you changing the subject on me?" Her arms wind around my neck and she slides onto my lap as natural as if she was made for this seat.

"Maybe." I can hear people around us laughing, talking, and discussing our conversation, but I don't give a damn. These people are my family, and hopefully soon Ava will join this family.

She kisses me again before looking me in the eye.

"Knuckles, I don't care if my dad likes you or not. I love you. I'll do whatever it takes to be with you, no matter what."

Mr. Snuggles wiggles a bit and whines. She giggles and I take him out and put him back in her pink dog tote. I know there's no way her rich Dad will approve of me. I'm a biker, not a lawyer, not a CEO, not some billionaire playboy with a yacht. Just a biker. Who loves to fight.

But I am in love with Ava. I will protect her from anyone that might want to hurt her, and I'll spend the rest of my life loving her like she deserves to be loved.

All around us the bets are beginning to die down and I notice conversations begin to ramp back up. Beers are flowing, shots are being passed around, fights are breaking out. This place might be crazy, but it's home.

"So who did you bet for?" I ask again, my voice low.

"Are you trying to change the subject again?" she asks, her eyes darting back and forth between mine. I shake my head.

"I really want to know." My money is on Bear. I know Haley has had her eye on him for a while now and he's had his on her, but they seem to be unable to just take that next step to be together.

"Joker," she says, so matter of fact I can't help but think I must have missed something.

I glance past her at Joker. "*Really?*"

She nods.

"What do you know that I don't?" I haven't even seen him with someone.

She lifts both shoulders. "It's just a hunch."

Just a hunch. "How much did you bet?"

"A thousand." She says as if that's nothing.

I laugh. "Do you think your dad would approve?" Given that betting is illegal and she's the most upstanding citizen I know, though she's been a lot more… *relaxed* since I met her. I haven't forgotten the pill stealing incident. Though I'm proud of her for that clever ruse.

"Probably not." She scans the room, then glances at me again. "But I don't see him here, do you?"

"Nope." And that is fine with me.

"I'm going to win." She's so sure of herself I get the feeling I'm missing something.

"Then let's make it interesting." I say. "If you're right, I'll do whatever you want. If I'm right, you marry me. Deal?"

Her eyes light up at my words. She leans in and whispers, "I'd have done it for hard anal if I lost and cuddles if I won. But yours is good too," she says with a laugh. "And both ways, I'd still win."

Fuck, I love this woman.

The End

Oh my goodness! I'm having so much fun writing about these Naughty Devils. I hope you love them too. More coming soon. I promise!

Make sure you sign up to my newsletter so you don't

miss out.
 Tilly xx

ABOUT THE AUTHOR

Tilly Pope writes dirty, hot and over the top instalove stories about possessive alpha males who know what they want. Always short, sometimes cheesy, always naughty, no cheating and a guaranteed happily ever after.

Tilly loves football, spanking and wine.

Find her at tillypope.com

facebook.com/authortillypope
instagram.com/authortillypope
amazon.com/author/tillypope